The Adventures of Penny and Tubs
The City on the Sea

by Marcie May
& Margaret Zerhusen

illustrated by Maggie Chamberlin

Headline Kids
an imprint of Headline Books, Inc.
Terra Alta, WV

Acknowledgments

They say it takes a village to raise a child! Well, it's the same for a dream.

I would like to thank all of my family and friends for all of their support, encouragement, and prayers while working on *Penny & Tubs*. But a special thanks to my friend, Betsy, who spent many hours reviewing drawings and reading and re-reading and for my mom for being my personal cheerleader when I needed it most; to my good friend, Susan Kay Wyatt, and her beautiful daughter Elizabeth, for lending their gifted voices to *The City on the Sea*; to my beautiful daughter Vonnie: The "Zany Mrs. Z" and co-author of the book; to my co-songwriter, Tina Feder, for lending her gifted musical talents, and of course my beautiful granddaughter Sophia and my rather large kitty Rusty for their inspiration for the characters. And of course, the amazing Maggie Chamberlin for helping me develop my loveable characters, Penny and Tubs, and for breathing life into her wonderful illustrations. But I give most of my thanks to the biggest dream-maker of all, "through Him I can do all things."

The Adventures of Penny and Tubs — The City on the Sea

by Marcie May and Margaret Zerhusen
illustrated by Maggie Chamberlin

copyright ©2013 Marcie May and Margaret Zerhusen

To order additional copies of this book, or
for book publishing information, or to contact the author:

Headline Kids
P. O. Box 52
Terra Alta, WV 26764

Tel: 800-570-5951
Email: mybook@headlinebooks.com
www.headlinebooks.com
www.headlinekids.com

Published by Headline Books
Headline Kids is an imprint of Headline Books

ISBN-13: 978-0-938467-61-8

Library of Congress Control Number: 2012950091

PRINTED IN THE UNITED STATES OF AMERICA

"Hi! My name is Penny and this is Tubs; he is my cat.

Tubs and I are best friends and do just about everything together.

We love to sing songs, eat chocolate chip pancakes, swing on our play set, and be silly."

"Meow. Meow, Meeeooooow!"

"Oh, that's right Tubs; I forgot to tell them about our adventures.

As Tubs said, our very most favorite thing to do is take adventures using our imaginations.

Tubs and I can fly to different cities, fight dragons, search for buried treasure, explore in the jungle, and travel to a magical playground under the sea!"

"So, what do you say? Are you ready to take an adventure with us today?"

"Let's go!"

It was a starry night and Tubs and I were getting ready for bed. After we were all snuggle-buggled up in our favorite pjs, Mama tucked us tight into bed. She gave us each a kiss on the head and whispered, "Sweet dreams, my darlings." We closed our eyes and began to dream of all of our favorite things: kittens, butterflies, big slides and swinging. Then something strange started to happen... Tubs and I felt like we were floating.

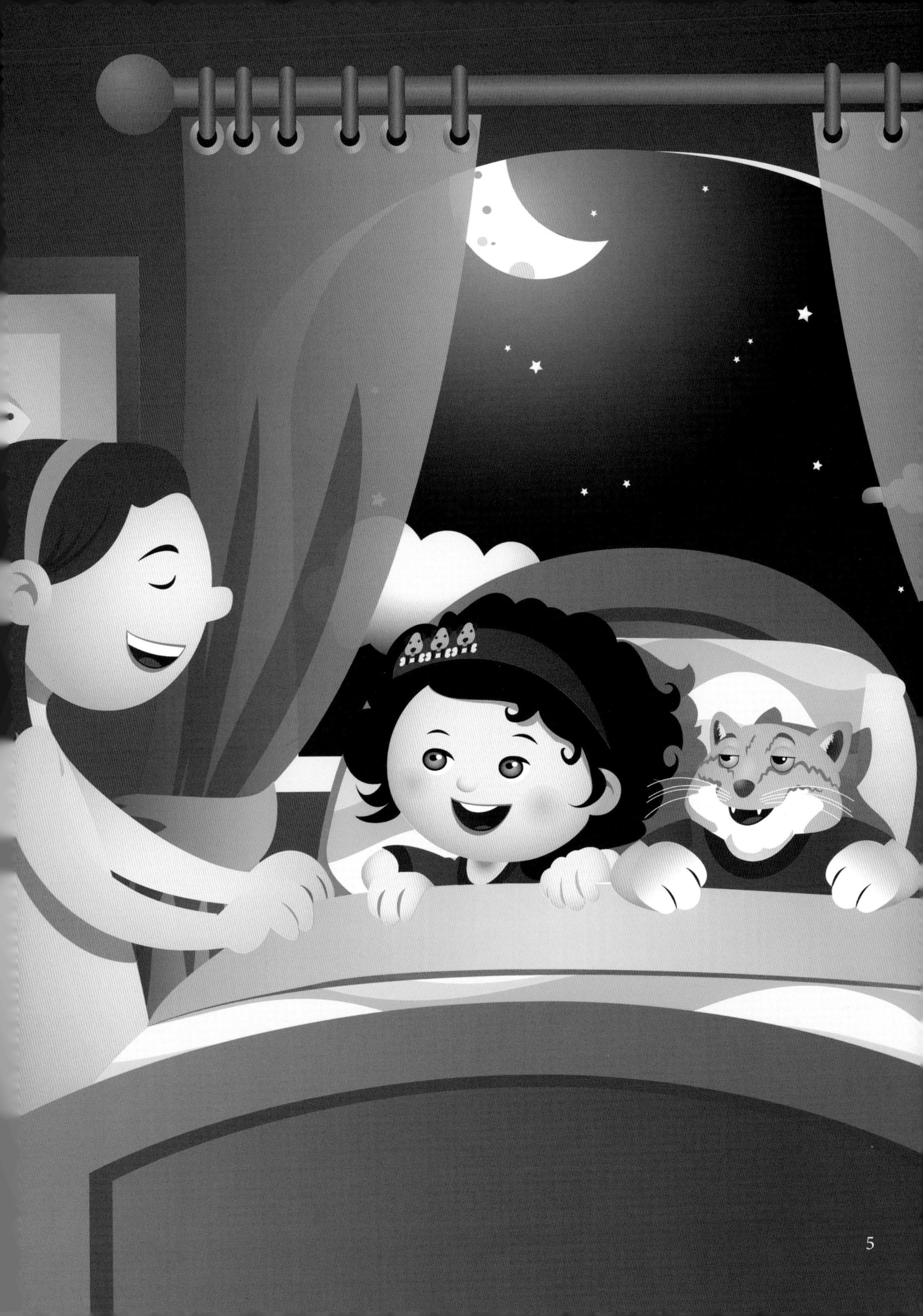

Tubs and I opened our eyes, only to discover we had floated to the ceiling, out of our bedroom and into the night sky! We were floating over the top of our house. At first we were scared, but then realized we were not just floating, we were flying. We could fly!

We flew across our yard into the night sky—going as high as we could go. "It's like pretending to fly on the swings but even better!" I yelled to Tubs. We flew so high and so far we finally did not know where we were.

I looked over and noticed Tubs was starting to get scared. I started to feel a little scared, too. I wondered if my mama knew we were gone, if she was worried about us, and if we were going to find our way home!

Then, we started to slow down. I looked at Tubs and just like that...we were falling. However, it was not a scary feeling. It was actually kind of fun. Tubs and I felt like we were zooming down our favorite slide at the park.

The faster we went, the tighter Tubs held onto me. I tried to see where we were going, but we were moving too fast! Then, with a soft thump, our feet landed on the ground and Tubs let out a long "MEOW."

"I wonder where we are," I said. "Let's take a look around!"

As we walked we could see houses floating on top of water. They were sparkling like blue glitter. I looked at Tubs and his eyes were wide with excitement. "Tubs, it looks like a city floating on the sea! We must go and explore everything, come on!" I yelled.

Tubs and I followed the boardwalk on which we had landed. We walked and walked and walked until finally Tubs perked up his ears. "What is it, Tubs? Do you hear something?" Tubs nodded his head and smiled. I listened as hard as I could and heard people singing. "Come on, Tubs, let's go!" I squealed.

We started running until we could see people who were laughing, singing, and dancing. Everyone seemed to be having so much fun and they all seemed to be singing the same song.

"Come with me to the city on the sea"
"Where being underwater is the place to be."

"It is a city on the sea, Tubs!" I said while dancing to the music. "Let's go see what else we can find."

Tubs and I continued our way down the boardwalk. We looked around and watched as the floating houses rocked gently back and forth. I smiled at Tubs and started to sing, *"Come with me to the city on the sea!"* As we looked closely, we could see the paint had peeled off some of the houses from the salty sea mist spraying up on the sides. It reminded me of the beach house we had seen on our summer vacation with Mama and Daddy.

As we kept walking, we soon came to what appeared to be the biggest house of all. It was white with bright blue shutters and a soft green roof. Tubs liked the house—I could tell. Before I could say no, Tubs decided to take a closer look and trotted up to the porch. We did not see anyone around and decided it would be okay to peek inside the window. The house was so big we had to stretch up tall to see inside.

On the inside, it looked very similar to our house, except there was a waterfall where the stairs should have been. "A waterfall for stairs?" I said to Tubs.

I loved the idea of sliding down a waterfall to get downstairs every day, but Tubs was not as excited. He scrunched up his pink nose and let out a short hiss in disagreement.

15

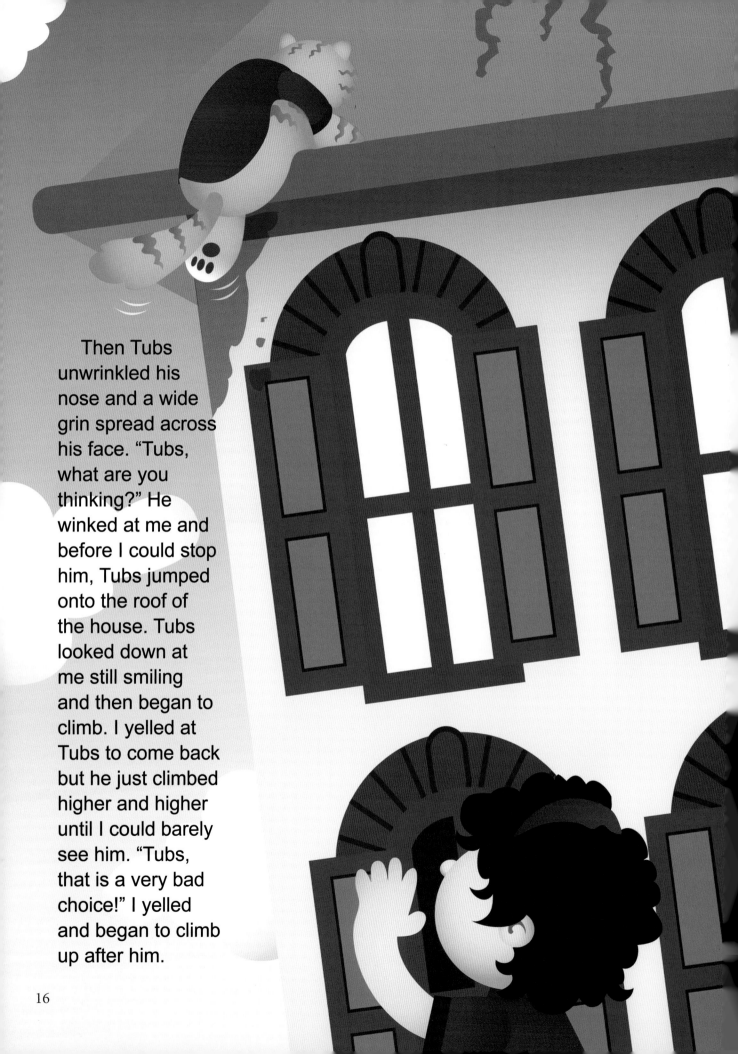

Then Tubs unwrinkled his nose and a wide grin spread across his face. "Tubs, what are you thinking?" He winked at me and before I could stop him, Tubs jumped onto the roof of the house. Tubs looked down at me still smiling and then began to climb. I yelled at Tubs to come back but he just climbed higher and higher until I could barely see him. "Tubs, that is a very bad choice!" I yelled and began to climb up after him.

The climb up to the roof was not as hard as I thought it would be and soon enough I joined Tubs at the very top. Now we could see the whole city. The city on the sea was even more beautiful from up high! It seemed to sparkle like a million stars in the night sky.

As we looked down from the house and into the clear blue water below, we could see children playing. Tubs and I smiled. We were so high up it was very hard to see everything that was going on but it looked like someone was waving at us. As I looked closer, I could see a boy waving and yelling at us. He seemed friendly so I decided to wave back.
"Come on in!" he yelled.

Suddenly, Tubs began slipping, causing both of us to fall off the roof and down we went into the water. When we splashed into the water, it was like landing on a giant, puffy marshmallow. "This city on the sea is full of surprises," I said to Tubs.

"Hi, I'm Adian," said the boy.
"Nice to meet you, Adian, My name is
Penny and this is Tubs. He's my cat."

20

I asked Adian where we were and how we got here. He just looked at me and laughed. This is the City on the Sea silly! You got here just like the rest of us, by making your way through the clouds." Tubs and I just looked at each other with puzzled expressions and Adian shook his head and smiled, "Come with me and let me show you the best part of the city!"

Adian took my hand and I grabbed Tubs, holding on to him as tight as I could. We dove down into the clear blue water and to our surprise we could breathe underwater just like fish! I looked over at Tubs and he was grinning all the way up to his whiskers.

We swam all the way down until our feet touched the bottom...it was sandy. We could not believe what our eyes saw! Here, at the bottom of the sea, was a big beautiful magical playground!

There was a merry-go-round with giant sea horses, clown fish, jellyfish, whales, and sharks—all swimming and playing with the children. There were slides, swings, a big carousel, monkey bars, and a giant colorful rainbow reaching from one end of the playground all the way to the other side.

It was unlike anything that Tubs and I had ever seen before. Just as we were deciding what to play on first, a pink and orange fish swam by and caught Tubs' attention. Tubs pushed off from the sandy bottom and started chasing after the silly-looking fish.

Adian and I swam over to the swings and climbed on. We began to swing as high as we could go, trying to make our toes touch a piece of the rainbow. The more we played, the more we forgot about home. This place was so magical, we started to feel like we never wanted to leave.

We had
been swinging for
what seemed only a little
while, but soon the sun began
to set and the rainbow began to
fade. One by one, all the children began
to leave until we were the only ones left.
Adian took my hand and I grabbed Tubs, and
together we swam back to where we had
begun our journey.

"Do we have to leave?" I asked Adian. "We just love it here!"

Adian started to laugh, "You can come back any time you want."

"But, I don't even know how we got here in the first place!" I said.

"Just close your eyes and believe," he said with a smile.

Just then, a big wave washed over us and pulled Tubs and I away. The wave pulled us farther and farther away from the city on the sea until we could not see it anymore. Tubs and I were so sleepy from our adventure that we closed our eyes and began to fall asleep.

After what seemed like a very short time, we opened our eyes and could hear Mama calling out to us, "Get up sleepy heads! It is time for breakfast!" We rubbed the sleep out of our eyes and took a deep breath. We could smell the sweet chocolate chip pancakes Mama had made and knew we were home. As fun as the city on the sea had been, it was very good to be home.

At breakfast I told Mama all about the city on the sea, Adian, and how Tubs went chasing after the funny-looking fish. She smiled and kissed Tubs and I on our heads. "It sounds like you had quite an adventure, but I am glad that you are home now." Tubs looked at me and let out a purr in agreement.

I know Mama thinks it was all just a dream,
but Tubs and I know the city on the sea is real. In
fact, Tubs and I are going back tonight and you
can come with us if you want! Remember, all you
have to do is close your eyes and believe.